THE STORY OF THE

HOUSTON
ROCKETS

CREATIVE EDUCATION

Published by Creative Education

123 South Broad Street

Mankato, Minnesota 56001

Creative Education is an imprint of The Creative Company.

DESIGN AND PRODUCTION BY **EVANSDAY DESIGN**

PHOTOGRAPHS BY Getty Images (Bill Baptist / NBAE, Andrew
D. Bernstein / NBAE, Nathaniel S. Butler, Scott Cunningham /
NBAE, Jim Cummins / NBAE, Focus on Sport, Sam Forencich /
NBAE, Jesse D. Garrabrant / NBAE, Glenn James / NBAE, Ronald
Martinez, Mike Powell, Rick Stewart, Noren Trotman, Rocky
Widner / NBAE)

LIBRARY OF CONGRESS CATALOGING-IN-PUBLICATION DATA

LeBoutillier, Nate.
The story of the Houston Rockets / by Nate LeBoutillier.
p. cm. — (The NBA—a history of hoops)
Includes index.
ISBN-13: 978-1-58341-408-8
1. Houston Rockets (Basketball team)—History—
Juvenile literature. I. Title II. Series.

GV885.52.H68L43 2006
796.323'64'097641411—dc22   2005051207

First edition

9 8 7 6 5 4 3 2 1

COVER PHOTO: *Tracy McGrady*

THE STORY OF THE
HOUSTON
ROCKETS

NATE LeBOUTILLIER

CREATIVE EDUCATION

Hakeem Olajuwon

ANCHORS HIMSELF CLOSE TO THE BASKET. HIS LONG FINGERS UNFURL TO CATCH THE BALL, AND A FAMILIAR FEELING COMES OVER HOUSTON FANS; THEY'VE SEEN THIS MANY TIMES. THE STAR CENTER CAN PASS IT—AND HE OFTEN DOES—TO A WIDE-OPEN TEAMMATE FOR AN EASY SCORE. BUT THIS TIME HE DECIDES TO GO WITH HIS SIGNATURE MOVE, THE "DREAM SHAKE." HIS SHOULDERS TWITCH, AND BEFORE THE DEFENDER KNOWS IT, OLAJUWON HAS FAKED, WHIRLED, AND LEFT THE GROUND FOR A GRACEFUL, FADING JUMP SHOT. THE BALL SPLASHES INTO THE NET. TWO POINTS, HOUSTON ROCKETS.

PREPARE FOR FLIGHT

1

HOUSTON, TEXAS, IS A CITY THAT COMBINES THE OLD and the new. The city was named in 1836 after General Sam Houston, who led the army that won Texas's independence from Mexico. The city of Houston's contributions to modern technology are equally obvious. Impressive skyscrapers form the heart of the city, and Houston is home to the Johnson Space Center—the headquarters for America's astronaut training program. In 1971, a National Basketball Association (NBA) team also moved to town. That team, fittingly, was named the Rockets.

The Rockets started out in San Diego, California. Added to the NBA in 1967, the Rockets didn't soar very high at first, finishing 15–67. But with the top pick in the 1968 NBA Draft, the team selected powerful young forward Elvin Hayes from the University of Houston.

9

ROCKETS

Elvin Hayes spent seven seasons with the Rockets—four at the start of his career, and three at the end

Although he was one of the NBA's shortest players, Calvin Murphy was extremely quick and fearless

The 6-foot-9 Hayes, known to fans as "The Big E," had a sensational rookie season, leading the NBA in scoring with 28 points and 17 rebounds per game. He boasted a turnaround jump shot that was virtually unstoppable, and he rebounded the ball like a wild man. "Rebounding is a rough proposition," he once noted. "But it's one of the ways I make my living, so it's something I force myself to tolerate, no matter how many bruises I wind up with."

In 1970, the Rockets drafted guard Calvin Murphy and forward Rudy Tomjanovich. Although just 5-foot-9, Murphy could score from anywhere on the court with his high-arcing jump shot. Tomjanovich had a soft jump shot and a knack for working the offensive boards and soon became a steadying influence on the Rockets.

Led by Hayes, Murphy, and Tomjanovich, the Rockets improved to 40–42 in 1970–71. In 1971, however, the team's owners decided to move the franchise to Houston due to low fan attendance in San Diego. After the 1971–72 campaign, the Rockets traded Hayes to the Baltimore Bullets.

Hayes's departure put a dent in the Rockets' metal, but a year later, the Rockets added two new sensational players: center Moses Malone and guard John Lucas. Malone gave Houston the potent scorer and rebounder it had been lacking, while Lucas was a gifted and confident ball handler and passer. "John doesn't overwhelm you with talent," said Rockets guard Mike Newlin. "He's just smooth. He asserts himself without infringing on anyone else's space, which is really an art."

Houston has a history of dominant centers, from Moses Malone to Ralph Sampson (pictured) to Yao Ming

THE PUNCH

On December 9, 1977, an ugly fight broke out between players from the Los Angeles Lakers and the Rockets. The Rockets' Rudy Tomjanovich was trying to act as peacemaker when powerful 6-foot-8 Lakers forward Kermit Washington swung his fist wildly, striking Tomjanovich. Washington's punch caused such damage to Tomjanovich's eye, cheek, and jaw that it nearly killed him. Tomjanovich made a comeback but was never the same player, although he went on to coach the Rockets to two NBA titles. Washington, who was suspended for two months by the NBA for the incident, still has trouble living down "the punch." "Rudy realizes that I'm sorry, and I'm glad that he's forgiven me," Washington said years later. "Maybe when I die, they won't have on my grave, 'The guy who hit Rudy Tomjanovich.'"

THIS NEW LINEUP LED HOUSTON ALL THE WAY TO the Eastern Conference Finals after the 1976–77 season. The Rockets seemed poised to go a step further the next year, but during a game against the Los Angeles Lakers midway through the season, a fight broke out, and Lakers forward Kermit Washington hit Tomjanovich with a staggering punch. Tomjanovich missed the rest of the season, and Houston finished 28–54.

In 1978–79, Tomjanovich was back, and Malone enjoyed perhaps his finest season. The big center averaged nearly 25 points and 18 rebounds per game to earn the NBA's Most Valuable Player (MVP) award. In addition, veteran guard Rick Barry joined the Rockets, giving the team another talented scorer. Houston made the playoffs but fell to the Atlanta Hawks in the first round.

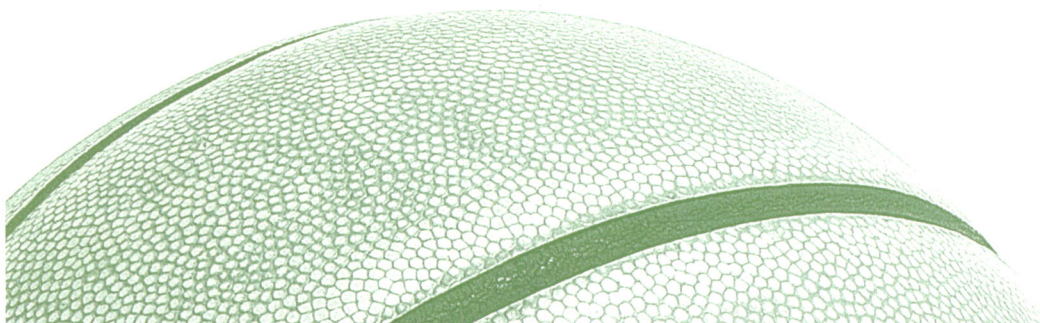

15

Moses Malone played for eight different teams in his NBA career but spent the most seasons in Houston

TROY

At a lean 6-foot-8, guard Robert Reid could easily rise above opponents to unleash his sweet jump shot

The Rockets posted mediocre records the next two seasons, but their 40–42 finish in 1980–81 was good enough to earn them a playoff berth. Once there, they stunned the league by reaching the NBA Finals. No one gave Houston much of a chance against Larry Bird and the Celtics, but the Rockets—behind Malone and guards Murphy and Robert Reid—won two games before losing the series. "Every member of our team can take great pride in playing on a team that people said wouldn't win a single playoff game," Coach Del Harris said.

Over the next few years, the Rockets' stars vanished one by one. In 1982–83, Houston fell to 14–68. Tomjanovich and Murphy had retired, and Malone was long gone to the Philadelphia 76ers. Never in their history had the Rockets been more in need of a boost.

PHI SLAMMA JAMMA REUNITED

For two years straight in the early 1980s, the University of Houston Cougars lost in the National Collegiate Athletic Association (NCAA) basketball championship game. Two members of the Houston squad—affectionately known as "Phi Slamma Jamma" because of their high-flying, dunk-loving nature—Akeem "The Dream" Olajuwon and Clyde "The Glide" Drexler went on to illustrious careers in the NBA. Olajuwon's Rockets won the 1994 NBA championship, and late in the 1994–95 season, Houston traded with the Portland Trail Blazers to bring Drexler back "home." Olajuwon and Drexler powered the Rockets through the playoffs and to a four-game sweep of the Orlando Magic in the 1995 Finals to finally give the reunited teammates a championship season together. "It was great to win the championship in the place where it all began," said Drexler.

3

HOUSTON'S WOEFUL RECORD GAVE THE TEAM THE first pick in the 1983 NBA Draft. The Rockets used the selection to take center Ralph Sampson, a three-time College Player of the Year from the University of Virginia. The team also plucked talented forward Rodney McCray from that year's draft.

McCray and the 7-foot-4 Sampson improved the Rockets, but their 29–53 record the next year was still the NBA's worst. "On the one hand, no team wants to be in the cellar," said Rockets coach Bill Fitch. "On the other hand, being in the cellar gives us a shot at number one in the draft again."

SAMPSON 50

HOUSTON 34

19

The "Twin Towers" of Ralph Sampson and Akeem Olajuwon were a scary sight to opposing shooters

ROCKETS

NBA 1985

Rodney McCray was a solid scorer in the late 1980s but was perhaps most valuable as a defender

After a lucky coin flip, the Rockets again won first choice in the NBA Draft.

Again they selected a center—this time 7-footer Akeem (later Hakeem) "The

Dream" Olajuwon from the University of Houston. In 1985–86, Sampson

and Olajuwon—the "Twin Towers,"—backed by McCray, Lucas, and guard

Lewis Lloyd, soared to a 51–31 mark. In the playoffs, the Rockets clinched

a spot in the NBA Finals on a beautiful last-second shot by Sampson in

Game 5 of the Western Conference Finals versus the Lakers. But the Boston

Celtics triumphed in six games to again dash Houston's title hopes.

The Rockets broke up the Twin Towers in 1987, trading Sampson to Golden

State and turning to Olajuwon to lead the way. Olajuwon boasted many

devastating moves in the low post, but none was as unstoppable as the

"Dream Shake," a spinning move that led to a fadeaway jump shot from

the baseline. "Olajuwon is blessed with grace, ability, and quickness…,"

marveled former Rockets guard Rick Barry. "His edge is his ability to outdo

his opponents physically: outjump, outquick, outrun them."

TWIN TOWERS

Lucky enough (or bad enough) to pick first in the NBA Draft in both 1983 and 1984, the Rockets decided to experiment. Ralph Sampson, a gigantic 7-foot-4 center out of the University of Virginia was their choice in 1983. The University of Houston's Akeem Olajuwon, another 7-footer who played center, was the pick in 1984. So what were the Rockets doing stockpiling two great players who played the same position? "I don't know a coach who would tell you that Olajuwon and Sampson can't play together in the same lineup," Coach Bill Fitch said. "Then again, we could cut them in half and make four guards." Fitch and the Rockets had the last laugh. In 1985–86, the "Twin Towers" led Houston all the way to the NBA Finals.

TWIN TITLES

4

THE ROCKETS FEATURED TOUGH POWER FORWARD Otis Thorpe and point guard Kenny Smith in the late 1980s, but the team played average basketball. In 1992, former Rockets star Rudy Tomjanovich was named head coach. In just his second season at the helm, Houston went 58–24 and soared into the 1994 playoffs.

With Michael Jordan off playing baseball, the Chicago Bulls—winner of the three previous championships—were weakened. The starting lineup of Olajuwon, Thorpe, Smith, guard Vernon Maxwell, and forward Robert Horry took advantage of the opportunity. Houston beat Portland, Phoenix, and Utah, and then battled past the New York Knicks in seven hard-fought games to claim its first NBA championship.

ROCKETS

Point guard Kenny Smith earned the nickname "The Jet" thanks to his speed and terrific leaping ability

Clyde Drexler engaged in some great battles with fellow star guard Michael Jordan of the Chicago Bulls

Midway through the next season, Houston added another offensive weapon by trading Thorpe to Portland for All-Star guard Clyde "The Glide" Drexler. The addition seemed a natural fit, since Drexler had grown up in Houston and played college ball with Olajuwon. The Rockets showed heart in making it past three 50-game winners to return to the Finals, and then they crushed the Orlando Magic in four straight games to repeat as champions. "We are a team of destiny," Olajuwon said. "That's the only way to explain it. You could see it coming."

After falling short in the playoffs in 1996, the Rockets traded for star forward Charles Barkley, giving Houston's lineup three future Hall-of-Famers. "We're going to cause some teams some problems," Barkley predicted. "You're not going to not double-team Hakeem, and you're not going to not double-team Clyde."

Barkley helped drive Houston as far as the Western Conference Finals in 1997, but the Utah Jazz then trumped them. Injuries led to a mediocre season the next year, and Drexler retired. To fill the void, Houston again traded for a veteran superstar—Chicago Bulls forward Scottie Pippen. But the sinking Rockets lost in the first round of the 1999 playoffs, and Pippen was soon traded to the Portland Trail Blazers.

MARIO ELIE, JOURNEYMAN SNIPER

One of the most famous shots in Rockets history came from an unexpected source. In Game 7 of a second-round playoff series in 1995, the Rockets and Phoenix Suns were tied. Rockets guard Mario Elie had the ball, and everyone in the Suns' arena expected him to throw it in to star center Hakeem Olajuwon. "Dream was wide-open, but I had my feet set," Elie said. "I let it go and it felt good." The shot rained through the net with 7.1 seconds remaining, and Elie blew the Suns' bench a good-bye kiss. The Rockets won 115–114 and went on to capture the NBA title. Elie played for 6 teams in his 11 NBA seasons but spent 4 years with the Rockets, where he was—and still is—loved like a native son.

With Hakeem Olajuwon, Charles Barkley, and Clyde Drexler in uniform, the Rockets were an NBA power

BLASTING INTO THE FUTURE

THE 1999–00 SEASON MARKED A CHANGING OF THE guard in Houston. Olajuwon was hurt, and a knee injury ended Barkley's career. Without these veterans leading the way, the Rockets' excellent run came to an end, and they missed the playoffs four seasons in a row.

Still, some talented players entertained Houston fans during those years. Explosive point guard Steve Francis and rapid-fire shooting guard Cuttino Mobley were not only close friends, but a difficult duo for opponents to handle. And in 2002, the Rockets made 7-foot-5 center Yao Ming from Shanghai, China, the first pick in the NBA Draft. Ming soon became a fan favorite in the United States as well as in China. "It will take time to adapt," said Ming on learning the NBA game, "but I think I can handle it."

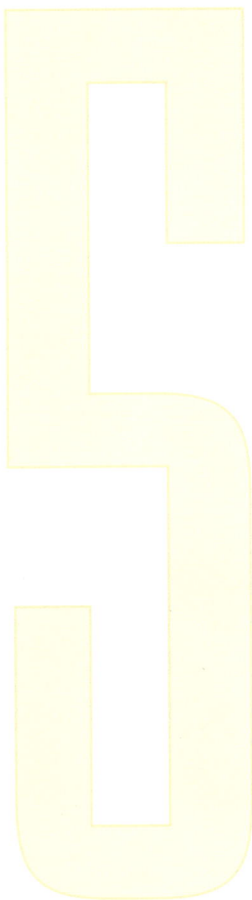

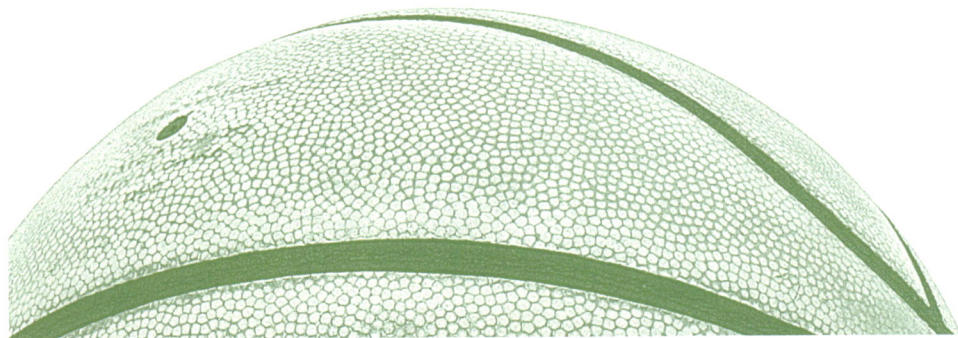

29

ROCKETS

A hero in his native China, giant center Yao Ming was an intimidating inside presence for the Rockets

Known to fans as "T-Mac," long-armed and high-flying forward Tracy McGrady was an electrifying scorer

NBA

After the 2003–04 season, in which the Rockets returned to the playoffs but lost in the first round, Francis and Mobley were traded to Orlando for sleek forward Tracy McGrady. McGrady, adept at playing both inside and out, had led the league in scoring the previous season and teamed up nicely with Ming under new head coach Jeff Van Gundy to give the Rockets a potent one-two punch. The Rockets won 51 games in 2004–05 and took the Dallas Mavericks to seven games in the playoffs before succumbing. "Our team had played well all year, but to crack like that in the biggest game of the year is disappointing," said Van Gundy following the Rockets' loss in Game 7.

Like the city of Houston, the Rockets have featured their share of skyscrapers over the years. From The Big E to "Mo" Malone to the Twin Towers to Yao Ming, Houston has always featured scintillating inside play. After witnessing the Rockets' back-to-back NBA championships in the 1990s, today's Rockets plan to launch themselves to more titles in the years ahead.

WITH FRIENDS LIKE BARKLEY...

Kenny "The Jet" Smith was a lightning-quick guard who played for the Rockets from 1990 to 1996. Colorful forward Charles Barkley joined the Rockets for the final four seasons of his career the season after Smith left. Although they never teamed up together for the Rockets, they have in the television studio, on the Turner Network Television (TNT) station where—with host Ernie Johnson—they have discussed NBA games and engaged in verbal warfare since 2000. "It's like when you have a championship team," said Smith of his job working with Barkley and Johnson. "There's a feeling when you walk into the building that something's different. This is something special." Barkley, as usual, was less complimentary, cracking to Johnson and Smith: "I'm the smartest person on this set. You two are just here for decorations."